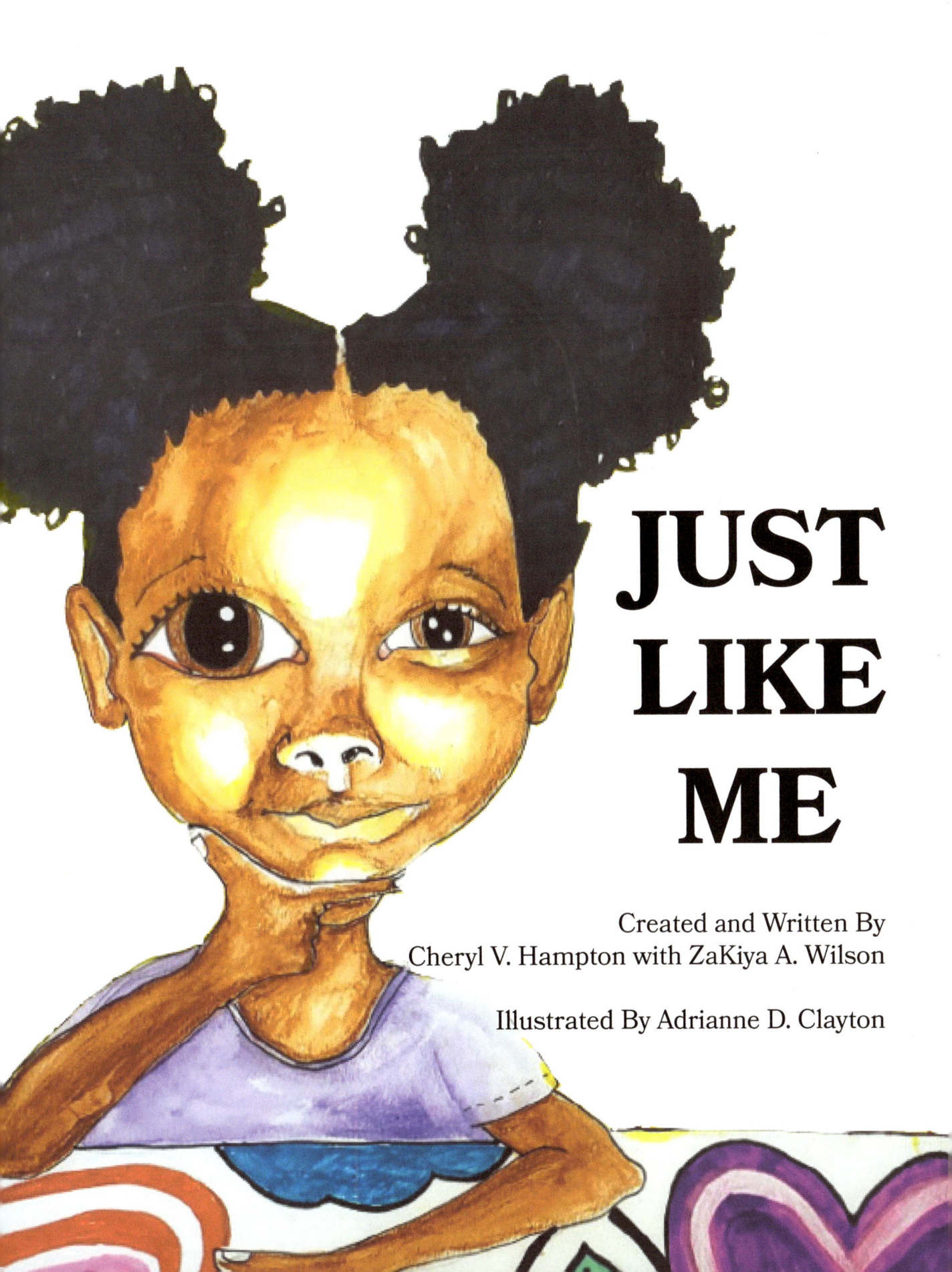

I would first like to thank Marty Galutia, for her steadfast support and encouragement with this endeavor.

Secondly, I would like to thank the PLTI (Parent Leadership Training Institute). Facilitators, Julie Holland, Nicole Jacobs-Silvey, Denesha Snell, Elizabeth Williams, and Crystal Everett, for providing me with the opportunity to fulfill a dream through my community class project.

Next, I would like to thank Joshua Q. Nickens, for his techinical assistance!

Last but not at all Least, to my grandchildren, Charlize R. Jackson, Kylie A. Brown, Monique R. Ray and Tyler R. Ray. You all have unlocked a door in my heart that I could have never imagine existed! When I look into your innocent eyes, full of curiosity and questions. I pray as your grandmother that I provide you with wise answers, in an effort to direct you to the righteous path of life, so that you may grow to be open-minded and love all mankind despite his/her differences.

A special thanks to my oldest granddaughter, Charlize R. Jackson who had to accompany me to PLTI class every Sunday, initially I did not realize your presence would be the inspiration for creating this book.

---

Just Like Me is a work of fiction. Names, characters, places, and incidents are either the productions of the author's imagination or are used fictitiously. Any resemblance to actual persons, living or dead, events, or locales is entirely coincidental.

Just Like Me
Written by Cheryl V. Hampton and ZaKiya A. Wilson

© 2020 Cheryl V. Hampton

ALL RIGHTS RESERVED. No part of this publication may be reproduced, distributed, or transmitted in any form or by any means, including photocopying, recording, or other electronic or mechanical methods, without the prior written permission of the authors. Contact the authors at:

cheryl.hampton47@gmail.com
zakiya.wilson@gmail.com

Library of Congress Control Number: 2020916155

ISBN: 978-1-735649207

Printed in the United States of America
10 9 8 7 6 5 4 3 2 1

First Edition

DEAR READERS,

LOOKING THROUGH THE LENS OF HER SIX YEAR OLD EYES TO UNDERSTAND HUMANITY DIFFERENCES.

**JUST LIKE ME**, IS A STORY ABOUT AN AFRICAN AMERICAN YOUNG GIRL NAMED CHARLIZE R. JACKSON, AND HER VISIT TO ANYTOWN.

FIND OUT WHAT CHARLIZE DISCOVERS IN "JUST LIKE ME," THE FIRST BOOK IN THE "EVERYONE IS SOMEONE." SERIES.

Cheryl V. Hampton

Today is a special day for Charlize and her Grandma Cheryl, she lovingly calls Maw Maw.

"Maw Maw, where are we going today?" Charlize asked.

"Somewhere extraordinary!" her Grandma exclaimed.

"Is it the park?"

"What about the Ice Cream parlor? I sure do love Ice Cream!"

"Oooh, Maw Maw, I know, we are going to the movies."

"No Charlize, not today. Now go and grab your jacket sweetheart and let's go!" Maw Maw replied.

Maw Maw and Charlize pulled
up in front of the big building,
called Any Town, a center that
provides housing and placement
for homeless and foster children of
different age, race and gender.

"Wow! Maw Maw where are we?
I have never been here before!"
Charlize said in amazement.

They got out of the car and went to
meet some very special people.

Charlize met a lot of new friends.
One of her friends name was Julie.
They played hop scotch, tag and
jumped rope together.

Julie's mom came over to meet Charlize and her grandma Cheryl. To Charlize's surprise, Julie's mom was black while Julie was white.

Charlize did not quite understand how was this possible!

After a fun filled day at Any Town, Charlize had a lot of questions for her grandma Cheryl. The car ride home was very interesting.

"Maw Maw how is Julie white, but her mom is black? Grandma, you're black and I am black, so when I grow up and get married, my husband and our children will be black, right?"

"Yes, that is very possible. Charlize, but what if you chose to marry someone of a different race?"

" What do you mean by race, Maw Maw? Like when I run track."

"No baby. Race is a concept that is used to distinguish different types of physical traits in people. Nonetheless, you do not have to worry about marriage for a long time, we will have plenty of time to talk about that and trust me Charlize, you're only six years old and your focus should be on school and learning all you can."

"Yes what is it Charlize?"

"I can do that?"

"Do What?" Maw Maw replied.

"I can marry someone a different color than me?"

"You sure can," Maw Maw smiled.

"Maw Maw, I have more questions, why is everyone in our neighborhood black? Are there all white neighborhoods?"

"I'm sure of it Charlize. Maw Maw replied.

"Wow! That's something else Maw Maw. But now Maw Maw we can live together and not be separated by the color of our skin!"

"Yes. That's right!"

"So why do we live in an all-black neighborhood?"

Maw Maw replied, "Well my sweet baby, there are many reasons. Hopefully I can explain, so that you can understand. Let's begin dinner and talk about it."

Charlize washed up for dinner and ran downstairs to sit at the dinner table, while Maw Maw cooked dinner and told the story of how it all got started.

"Okay Maw Maw I'm ready to hear the story," Charlize said eagerly.

"Once upon a time, a number of years ago, there was a man named Jesse Clyde Nichols, better known as J.C. Nichols. To make a long story short, he developed special neighborhoods that separated people of color, commonalities and currency."

"You mean money, Maw Maw?"

"Yes, Charlize. So, it wasn't always easy for people of color to live where they wanted to live. We often had to live in designated and/or poorly developed neighborhoods for blacks only! Called Colored back in those days. See neighborhoods weren't designed with blacks in mind. Now, even though we're able to live in some of those formerly restricted areas today, there are certain circumstances such as affordability, which is a more sophisticated way of limiting people of color's access to live in certain neighborhoods.

"Maw Maw is this a make-believe story?"

"No Charlize, unfortunately this story is true."

"Well that's too bad because I believe everybody would love to live by me!"

"Yes, they would," Maw Maw said as she served dinner.

After dinner, Charlize went to take her bath, brushed her teeth and put on her pajamas.

Tucking Charlize in was one of Maw Maw's favorite things to do. Maw Maw gave Charlize a big hug.

"Maw Maw you give the BEST hugs ever!"

After praying, Charlize jumped into the bed. Maw Maw said, "good night my sweet girl."

"Maw Maw wait! You still didn't answer my first question. How is Julie white and her mom is black?"

Maw Maw sat on the bed, "Well Charlize due to unfortunate circumstances, Julie's biological parents could not care for her, so they did the second-best thing, which was contact Children's Social Services for guidance. Now she is with someone despite the color of their skin who will love and provide care for her in a stable and safe environment."

"So, Maw Maw, Julie is Just Like Me."

"What do you mean Charlize?"

"Well you help take care of me."

"Yes, I do because I love you and that's what families do! Related or Unrelated. Now go to sleep." Maw Maw said as she kissed Charlize on the forehead. "It is past your bedtime."

Charlize smiled and whispered, "Maw Maw how did Children's Social Services choose Julie's mom?"

"We will talk about being *Uniquely Placed*, tomorrow. Okay my sweet girl?"

"Okay Maw Maw."

It is my hope that this little book can help parents/families begin speaking with their young children honestly about race related moments. And the true beauty of us all being a part of one Human Family. Creating Humanities Rainbow, which reveals colors that represent all people! Black, Red, Yellow, Brown and White, teaching the true virtue of humanity.

LOVE

---

Remember love is patient, love is kind, it does not envy, it does not boast, it is not proud. It does not dishonor others, it is not self-seeking, it is not easily angered. It keeps no record of wrongs. Love does not delight in evil but rejoices with the truth. It always protects, always trusts, always hopes, always perseveres.

LOVE NEVER FAILS

NIV:1Corinthians 13: 4-8

## About the Author

Cheryl Hampton, is an author, storyteller, and social justice advocate. Her signature stories, "The Stamp" (Sent.To.Achieve.My.Purpose), and "Connecting the Dots of Life," are captivating and touch the core of the heart. She has a heart for those that the world considers not worth much! As the Founder of Big Hoops Production,  she has created a platform for the Underdog to share and rewrite their story and embrace the deeper truth! That only while there's Hope is there Life.

---

"There Can be no Keener Revelation of a Society's Soul than the way In which It Treats Its Children"

-Nelson Mandela

CPSIA information can be obtained
at www.ICGtesting.com
Printed in the USA
LVHW051002170920
666329LV00005B/45